"I DON'T LIKE CHOOSE YOUR OWN ADVENTURE® BOOKS. I *LOVE* THEM!" says Jessica Gordon, age ten. And now, kids between the ages of six and nine can choose their own adventures too. Here's what kids have to say about the Skylark Choose Your Own Adventure® books.

"These are my favorite books because you can pick whatever choice you want—and the story is all about you."
—**Katy Alson,** *age 8*

"I love finding out how my story will end."
—**Joss Williams,** *age 9*

"I like all the illustrations!"
—**Savitri Brightfield,** *age 7*

"A six-year-old friend and I have lots of fun making the decisions together."
—**Peggy Marcus** *(adult)*

Bantam Skylark Books in the Choose Your Own
   Adventure® Series
Ask your bookseller for the books you have missed

HAUNTED HARBOR

SHANNON GILLIGAN

ILLUSTRATED BY BILL SCHMIDT

An R.A. Montgomery Book

A BANTAM SKYLARK BOOK®
TORONTO · NEW YORK · LONDON · SYDNEY · AUCKLAND

RL 2, 007–009

HAUNTED HARBOR

A Bantam Skylark Book / April 1986

CHOOSE YOUR OWN ADVENTURE ® is a registered trademark of Bantam Books, Inc. Registered in U.S. Patent and Trademark Office and elsewhere.

Original conception of Edward Packard

Skylark Books is a registered trademark of Bantam Books, Inc. Registered in U.S. Patent and Trademark Office and elsewhere.

ISBN 0-553-15380-3

Published simultaneously in the United States and Canada

Bantam Books are published by Bantam Books, Inc. Its trademark, consisting of the words "Bantam Books" and the portrayal of a rooster, is Registered in U.S. Patent and Trademark Office and in other countries. Marca Registrada. Bantam Books, Inc., 666 Fifth Avenue, New York, New York 10103.

PRINTED IN THE UNITED STATES OF AMERICA

CW   0 9 8 7 6 5 4 3 2

HAUNTED HARBOR

READ THIS FIRST!!!

Most books are about other people.

This book is about you—and the ghost of English Harbor.

What happens to you depends on what you decide to do. Do not read this book from the first page straight through to the last page. Instead, start on page one and read until you come to your first choice. Then turn to the page shown and see what happens. When you come to the end of a story, go back to the beginning and start a new adventure!

What will happen when you meet the ghost? You're about to find out.

Good luck!

Vacation is finally here. This year you and **1** your parents are sailing around the Caribbean Sea! Your two best friends from school, Jamie and Meg, have been invited along too.

Almost every day you sail to a new island. But for three nights your boat is anchored at English Harbor, on an island called Antigua.

As soon as you get there, the three of you head straight for the beach to play with the island kids.

"What's it like around here?" you ask them.

One of them answers, "It's pretty nice, but whatever you do, don't go near the old cemetery on the hill after dark. It's haunted. Old folks say the ghost of English Harbor lives there."

Another kid says, "People have gone in there at night and never come out!"

Turn to page 2.

2 You watch as the kids leave. "I wonder if they were telling the truth?" Meg says.

"Well, *I* believe in ghosts," Jamie replies.

"So do I," Meg agrees.

"*Ghosts?*" you laugh. "You two must be kidding!"

"No, we're not," Jamie says. "If you're so sure there's no ghost of English Harbor, why don't you go to the cemetery to find out? We *dare* you!"

You look at your two friends. "Tonight?" you ask.

Meg and Jamie nod.

"Okay," you say boldly. "I'll go!"

Turn to page 9.

You peek quickly around the bushes. **5** There's a dark, narrow cave in the side of the hill. The laughter is coming from inside!

Maybe you've discovered someone's hide-out! You take a step into the cave to listen more closely.

Inside it's pitch-dark. You feel oddly light, as if you're floating. You try to walk, but there's no ground under your feet!

Then—THUNK! You feel the earth under your feet again. You run out of the cave.

It's daylight! What just happened? Only a minute ago it was night. Did you fall asleep?

Turn to page 10.

6   You jump to your feet and tear up the beach as fast as you can. But the white mist catches up and surrounds you. Invisible icy hands grab your shoulders and pin you down!

"Who are you?" you cry wildly. "What do you want?"

"I am the ghost of English Harbor," a heavy voice answers. "I need your help."

Turn to page 18.

That night you wait until your parents are asleep. Then the three of you sneak out of bed and go up on deck.

You stare into the inky black water with a weak feeling in your stomach. What if Meg and Jamie are right? It's too late to back out on the dare now. Maybe you could just pretend to go to the cemetery? You could hide somewhere for a few hours and *tell* them you went.

But wait a minute! What are you thinking? There *is* no such thing as ghosts!

Or is there?

If you decide to go to the cemetery even though you're scared, turn to page 13.

If you decide to hide someplace for a few hours and make up a story about the ghost for Jamie and Meg, turn to page 14.

10   You look down at the harbor, but all the boats are gone. All the buildings have disappeared too! In the distance you can see Boggy Peak, the tallest mountain on Antigua. At least you're on the same island. But why has everything changed?

Suddenly you hear more laughter. This time it's closer. You turn around. The noise is coming from a group of five men down on the beach.

Their skin is painted bright red. Their black hair is long, shiny, and flowing. They have huge black circles painted around each eye, and they look very mean.

If you go up to the men and ask them to explain where you are, turn to page 29.

If you keep quiet to watch what they do next, turn to page 25.

You're going to go into the cemetery—ghost or no ghost. You whisper good-bye to Jamie and Meg. Then you lower your raft into the dark water and paddle toward the beach across the bay.

When you get there, you hide the raft in some bushes. You can see the old path up the hill. The cemetery is at the top.

You feel a bit scared. The bushes and trees look like huge, scary insects. But at least the moon is bright.

You walk along briskly. Everything is very quiet. Then, all of a sudden, you hear a laugh coming from behind a clump of bushes. You stop to listen. There's something strange about the laughter. It has an echo!

If you go to see where the laughter is coming from, turn to page 5.

If you screw up your courage and continue to the cemetery, turn to page 16.

14 You decide to hide somewhere, but you get into your raft to leave as if nothing has changed. Meg and Jamie hang over the ship's rail watching you paddle off.

"If I'm not back by midnight, get the police!" you call to them.

You reach the beach across the bay and pull the raft up onto the sand. Then you settle in to wait under a tree.

You lie there staring at the stars. Suddenly things get very quiet. Even the crickets stop chirping.

You look up. An eerie white mist is moving up the beach toward you.

It's the ghost!

Turn to page 6.

16 The quicker you get this visit to the cemetery over with, the better. You can see who's laughing later.

Soon you arrive at the cemetery. The tombstones cast dark shadows in the moonlight. Other than that, it doesn't seem too scary. Sitting down, you look at your watch. You decide to give this ghost half an hour.

Five minutes later a tall white figure at the end of the cemetery catches your eye. Is it the ghost? You hide behind one of the tombstones to get a better look. As the figure passes between two rows, you see your mother's initials trailing along the ground.

That's no ghost! It's Meg and Jamie out to scare you with your mom's sheets!

If you decide to scare Meg and Jamie yourself, turn to page 22.

If you decide to ignore them and wait to see if the real ghost appears, turn to page 52.

18 The ghost's strange voice continues, "Hundreds of years ago I was a British soldier at the fort on this hill. I was killed by some Carib Indians during an attack. They chopped off my head. Then they buried my body in another place."

The ghost's voice rises to an angry shout. "My spirit will not be free until my skull and skeleton are back together!"

"What do you want me to do?" you wail.

"My skull is in the museum across the bay. Go there tomorrow and retrieve it," the ghost orders. "Bring it here tomorrow night!"

If you say, "Okay, I'll get the skull,"
turn to page 26.

If you say, "I'm just a kid. I can't help!"
turn to page 36.

You worry all day long. Your mom thinks you're sick. She makes you go to bed early. You don't dare tell her the truth.

That night there's a terrible storm in English Harbor. Many boats are damaged, including your parents'.

"We'll be here a few days longer than we thought," your father tells you. "We have to fix the boat."

Later you hear him tell your mother, "That storm was the strangest thing. It came out of nowhere and didn't go anywhere else. A mile away, it was calm and clear all night!"

You get a sinking feeling in your stomach. What will the ghost of English Harbor do next?

The End

The next day you learn that Hatu is the village shaman. He practices medicine and magic for the Arawaks. He introduces you to the whole tribe.

The Arawaks look scary, but they are very gentle. During the next few months they teach you many things. You learn how to catch fish with poison made from plants and how to build canoes out of logs. You even learn how to weave hammocks to string up in the huts.

One day Hatu, who is your special friend, says, "Tonight the moon is right for you to return to your own time. You will not have the chance again for six months. Tell me your choice by nightfall."

You go off alone to think. It's so hard to decide! You've missed your family very much. But you love it here, too.

If you stay for six more months,
turn to page 30.

If you decide to leave tonight,
turn to page 35.

"*I* know who's going to get the scare," you think. You sneak toward Meg and Jamie. But you trip on a rock. You go flying through the air and land—right in a freshly dug grave! Yuck!

You look up and see Meg's and Jamie's faces over the edge. They're both laughing so hard they can't talk. Finally Meg says, "Some ghost you'd make!" Then they laugh even harder.

You're so mad that you never want to speak to them again. But you have to. The only way to get out of the grave is by using your mother's sheets.

The End

You stay hidden in the bushes and watch **25** the five men from the hill. They talk and laugh together a short while more. Then they disappear into the forest.

You try to follow them. But you lose your way in a maze of forest trails. The sun is very hot. Your mouth feels dry and sticky. You begin to run. You've got to find water!

Finally you come to a small clearing filled with thatched huts. You stumble out of the forest. "Water!" you gasp. Then you pass out.

Turn to page 40.

26 "I'm glad you've decided to help," the ghost says in a horrible voice. "Meet me here tomorrow night. Don't forget the skull, or you'll be sorry!"

Slowly the mist travels back down the beach. Then it disappears.

You paddle back to your boat as fast as you can. Meg and Jamie are waiting up for you.

Meg says, "Well, did you see the ghost?"

"Tell us what happened!" Jamie begs.

If you decide to tell them everything, turn to page 51.

If you decide you have enough on your hands trying to get the skull by yourself, turn to page 32.

You start to run down the hill toward the men. But you trip over some vines and hit your head.

The next thing you know, you're waking up inside a thatched hut. An old man and two old women kneel on the ground next to you. They have red painted skin just like the men at the beach.

"Look," one of them says. "The god is awake!"

"It's just like my dreams," the other woman says. "For many nights I dreamed that a new god would come."

What's going on here? These people seem to think you're a god!

Turn to page 45.

30 You go back to the village and find Hatu. "I've decided to stay for six more months," you tell him.

Hatu smiles. "I thought you might," he says. "I am happy. Our tribe is very fond of you."

Life with the Arawaks goes on. Before you know it, three more months have passed. But one morning something happens to change everything. An old-fashioned sailing ship appears on the horizon. You remember seeing ships like it in a book back home in school.

The Arawaks are very excited. When the ship pulls into their bay, they run down the beach. They shout, "Peace! Peace! Peace!"

A man comes to the front of the ship. He shouts back, "I am Christopher Columbus. I have come to discover the New World!"

Turn to page 54.

32   It will be enough work to get the skull by yourself. So you lie to your friends.

"No, of course I didn't see the ghost," you tell Meg and Jamie. "There *is* no ghost!"

That night you can't sleep. You have nightmares about being strangled by an icy pair of hands. You are in no shape to grab the skull the next day, but you have no choice.

There's only one skull in the museum. It's on the second floor. You buy a ticket and walk around pretending you're part of a tour. Then you sneak into the room where the skull is in a glass case.

You make sure the guard is in another room, and then you lift up the glass cover. You're reaching in for the skull when a voice behind you booms, "Stop right where you are!"

Turn to page 46.

You think for a long time about whether to go back home. Finally you find Hatu and say, "It's hard to choose. But I think that now is the time for me to return."

Hatu nods sadly. "Come with me," he says.

You follow him as he walks into the forest. An hour later, you reach the cave on the hill. It is dark. A full moon rises over Boggy Peak in the distance.

"Before you go," Hatu says, "I want you to take something."

He presses a small carved shell into your hand. "This is the image of our most important god. He will guide you on a safe journey back to your own world," Hatu tells you. "Hold onto him tightly and step into the cave."

You turn to thank Hatu, but he's gone. With a lump in your throat, you walk forward into the darkness.

Turn to page 44.

"WHAT? YOU WON'T HELP?" The ghost bellows. "I'LL SHOW YOU!"

The last thing you remember is his icy hands throwing you twenty feet into the air.

You wake up in the hospital. Your leg and arm are broken. Your parents stare into your face as you open your eyes.

"Mom! Dad! What happened?" you ask.

"We were going to ask *you* that," your father says.

"I saw the ghost of English Harbor," you say. "He threw me into the air because I wouldn't steal his skull from the museum!"

Your parents look at each other and grin. Then your father pats your cast. "We didn't know that you hit your head, too!" he says.

The End

38   "I don't care what that ghost said," you tell Meg. "I'm with you. Let's get rid of this thing right now!"

The three of you paddle the raft back to where you met the ghost last night. You place the skull in the white sand under a lime tree. From a distance it blends right in.

"No one would notice the skull unless they were looking for it," Jamie says.

You are about to get back into the raft when Meg shouts, "Look!"

You glance up just in time to see a crab scurry across the sand and right inside the skull. There's a flash of blinding white light and a puff of smoke. The smoke slowly takes the shape of a man wearing a soldier's uniform. He runs down the beach to you.

"Thank you, thank you," he says. "I knew you would return my skull."

"But—but—I thought you were going to return to the spirit world!" you say.

"I am!" the ghost replies before he dives into the water. "I'm just going to have a swim first!"

The End

40   You wake up at dusk inside one of the huts. You are lying in a hammock. An old man is sitting on the ground next to you. He hands you a coconut shell filled with cool water.

"Who are you? Where am I?" you ask.

"I am an Arawak Indian. My name is Hatu. We are the people who live here on Walaadli," he answers gently.

"Walaadli? What happened to Antigua?" you cry.

The old man smiles and says nothing. In seconds you are fast asleep.

Turn to page 21.

You look at Meg and Jamie in horror. But
there's nothing to do.

Five minutes later you're sailing out of English Harbor. But you never make it to Nevis. Your ship disappears mysteriously somewhere on the short trip. No one ever sees you again.

The End

42 The next day your plan works perfectly. The skull is in an unlocked glass case. With Jamie on watch, you reach in and slip the skull into Meg's beachbag. Meg hides it under the towel. Then the three of you just stroll out!

"What do we do now?" Jamie asks as soon as you're out of sight.

"Why don't we leave the skull off at the beach during the day?" Meg suggests. "We can put it under a lime tree. The ghost will be able to find it."

You like Meg's idea. But you remember the ghost's words: "Meet me here tomorrow night . . . or you'll be sorry." If you don't show up in person, who knows what he'll do?

If you decide to put the skull under the tree, turn to page 38.

If you decide to wait till tonight, turn to page 50.

44   Inside the cave, you have the same floating feeling as before. In a few seconds you're back outside the cave. You see that the harbor is full of boats. Lights twinkle in the distance. You run down the hill, find your raft, and paddle back to your parents' boat.

Meg and Jamie are waiting up for you.

"What happened?" they whisper.

"I was on my way to the cemetery," you explain, "but a funny thing happened. I found a cave behind a clump of bushes. When I walked inside, I went back in time to when Arawak Indians lived on this island. I've been gone for months!"

"No, you haven't," replies Jamie. "You've been gone half an hour!"

"If you don't believe me, look at this," you say, showing them the carved shell Hatu gave you. "One of the Arawaks gave it to me. I'll show you the cave tomorrow."

Turn to page 49.

You sit up. "Wait a minute," you say. "I'm no god. I'm just a kid! Now, I don't know who you are or where I am. But I *do* know I have to get home fast or my parents are going to find me missing. Can you help me?"

The old man smiles strangely. "I know the way you came," he says. "You have been sent to us by the gods. To let you go would make them angry. No, now you must stay with us."

You don't know what's happening. But you're beginning to think it will be a while before you see your parents again.

The End

46   A guard is walking toward you. "What do you think you're doing?" he says.

"I just wanted a better look!" you cry.

"I could arrest you for this," says the guard. He stares you in the eye.

"Please," you start to explain, "I didn't mean any harm. I was just . . ."

"I don't want to hear it," the guard interrupts. "Just leave. And don't let me see you around here again."

Back outside you are miserable. Now your chances of getting the skull back are ruined!

Turn to page 19.

The next day you row the raft back over to **49**
the beach and lead Meg and Jamie up the hill
to the clump of bushes. But when you get
there, the cave is gone! There's only a dark
shadow where its mouth once was.

"Where did you say you found that carved
shell again?" Meg asks, smiling.

The End

50   "No, the ghost told me to return the skull tonight," you tell Jamie and Meg. "I'd better do what he said."

With nothing else to do, the three of you go back to your boat to wait. Your parents are both on deck getting ready to sail.

You climb on board. "I didn't know we were going out for a sail," you say.

"We're not," your father replies. "We've been invited to spend the night on an island called Nevis. I was just about to come find you kids."

"But I don't want to go!" you plead. You know you can't tell the truth.

"Don't be silly," your dad says. "You'll love Nevis. It's even prettier than Antigua."

Turn to page 41.

51

"I sure *did see* the ghost," you tell Jamie and Meg. "And I'm in trouble! The ghost wants me to bring his skull to him. It's in the museum. I have to meet him tomorrow night."

"What are you going to do?" cries Meg. Jamie is too scared to say anything.

"I've got a plan. But I'll need your help," you say.

"You can count on me," Meg answers.

"M-m-m-me too!" Jamie stutters.

"Good," you say. "Here's my plan. We'll all go to the museum in the morning. I think the skull is in a room on the second floor. Jamie, you'll stand guard at the door. Meg, you'll bring your beachbag with a towel in it. I'll take care of the rest. Got it?"

Meg and Jamie nod.

"Now let's get some sleep," you tell them.

Turn to page 42.

52 For the next few minutes you watch Jamie and Meg. They keep walking nearby. But you keep ignoring them. You can just feel them getting desperate to scare you.

All of a sudden you notice a white mist moving slowly across the cemetery in your direction. As it gets closer, you can make out its shape. It's a man in some kind of uniform—but he has no head!

"Meg! Jamie!" you scream without thinking. "It's the real ghost. Let's get out of here!"

You run down the path without looking back. As soon as you reach the beach, you launch your raft. A few seconds later, Meg and Jamie stumble down the path.

They run toward the raft, but you stand in the way. "A ride back to the boat is going to cost you two jokers a dollar apiece!"

The End

54 Christopher Columbus! You can't believe it! You're going to see one of the great moments in history! Wait till you get home and tell everyone!

But you never have the chance. Christopher Columbus forces you and the Arawaks to become his slaves.

You remember what your teacher once said: explorers were often very cruel to the people they met in the New World. But you never guessed that you would be one of those people!

The End

ABOUT THE AUTHOR

Shannon Gilligan graduated from Williams College in 1981. While a student, she spent a year studying at Doshisha University in Kyoto, Japan. Ms. Gilligan is also the author of *The Search for Champ, The Three Wishes, Mona Is Missing,* and *The Fairy Kidnap* in the Bantam Skylark Choose Your Own Adventure series. When she's not traveling to research her books, she lives in Warren, Vermont.

ABOUT THE ILLUSTRATOR

Bill Schmidt earned a BFA degree at Hartford Arts School in Hartford, Connecticut. He has illustrated a number of paperback books for children, including a series about robots. Mr. Schmidt has also illustrated many adult books and advertisements. The artist currently lives in Boonton Township, New Jersey.

CHOOSE YOUR OWN ADVENTURE

SKYLARK EDITIONS

☐	15226	Jungle Safari #13 E. Packard	$1.95
☐	15442	The Search For Champ #14 S. Gilligan	$2.25
☐	15444	Three Wishes #15 S. Gilligan	$2.25
☐	15465	Dragons! #16 J. Razzi	$2.25
☐	15489	Wild Horse Country #17 L. Sonberg	$2.25
☐	15262	Summer Camp #18 J. Gitenstein	$1.95
☐	15490	The Tower of London #19 S. Saunders	$2.25
☐	15501	Trouble In Space #20 J. Woodcock	$2.25
☐	15283	Mona Is Missing #21 S. Gilligan	$1.95
☐	15418	The Evil Wizard #22 A. Packard	$2.25
☐	15306	The Flying Carpet #25 J. Razzi	$1.95
☐	15318	The Magic Path #26 J. Goodman	$1.95
☐	15467	Ice Cave #27 Saunders/Packard	$2.25
☐	15342	The Fairy Kidnap #29 S. Gilligan	$1.95
☐	15463	Runaway Spaceship #30 S. Saunders	$2.25
☐	15508	Lost Dog! #31 R. A. Montgomery	$2.25
☐	15379	Blizzard of Black Swan #32 Saunders/Packard	$2.25
☐	15380	Haunted Harbor #33 S. Gilligan	$2.25
☐	15399	Attack of the Monster Plants #34 S. Saunders	$2.25
☐	15416	Miss Liberty Caper #35 S. Saunders	$2.25
☐	15449	The Owl Tree #36 R. A. Montgomery	$2.25
☐	15453	Haunted Halloween Party #37 S. Saunders	$2.25
☐	15458	Sand Castle #38 R. A. Montgomery	$2.25
☐	15477	Caravan #39 R. A. Montgomery	$2.25
☐	15492	The Great Easter Bunny Adventure #40 E. Packard	$2.25
☐	15509	The Movie Mystery #41 S. Saunders	$2.25

Prices and availability subject to change without notice.